This book belongs to

_____

_____

_____

In memory of Nana and Pop
—C.F.

To Ellie and Bethany, with love
—R.T.

tiger tales
5 River Road, Suite 128, Wilton, CT 06897
First published in the United States
by Abrams Books for Young Readers 2003
This paperback edition published
in the United States 2013
Originally published in Great Britain 2003
by Little Tiger Press
Text copyright © 2003 Claire Freedman
Illustrations copyright © 2003 Rory Tyger
CIP data is available
ISBN-13: 978-1-58925-440-4
ISBN-10: 1-58925-440-6
Printed in China
LTP/1400/1554/0416
3 5 7 9 10 8 6 4 2

For more insight and activities,
visit us at www.tigertalesbooks.com

Good Night, Sleep Tight!

by Claire Freedman

Illustrated by

Rory Tyger

tiger tales

One night, Ethan just could
not fall asleep.

"Aren't you sleepy, Ethan?"
asked Mommy.

"No," replied Ethan. "I don't
feel sleepy at all. I'm wide
awake!"

"Do you have your favorite
friends to cuddle up with?" she
asked. "They might help you
fall asleep."

"I have Tiger and Rabbit," said
Ethan. "But where's Elephant?"
"Here he is," said Mommy,
tucking him in nice and snug.
"Now you'll feel sleepy." But neither
Ethan nor his little friends went
to sleep.

"We're still wide awake,
Mommy," he said.
"What about a cup
of nice warm milk?"
said Mommy. "That makes
me sleepy."

Ethan drank every drop of his warm milk. But he didn't feel sleepy.

"I'm still wide awake, Mommy," he said. "Can we watch the fireflies? They might make me sleepy."

Mommy wrapped Ethan in his cozy blanket, and together they watched the dancing fireflies. Ethan tried to count them, but they didn't make him feel sleepy.

"I'm still wide awake, Mommy," he said. "Would you sing me a lullaby, please? That might make me tired."

Mommy sang some of
Ethan's favorite songs. Ethan
closed his eyes and listened . . . but he
didn't feel sleepy.

"I'm still wide awake," he whispered.

"I know, Ethan," Mommy said.
"Let me rock you in my arms. That
will make you sleepy."

Mommy rocked Ethan gently
in her arms, all the way down to
the apple orchard and back.

Ethan felt safe and warm,
but he didn't feel the
tiniest bit sleepy.

"Mommy, I'm STILL wide awake!"
he said. "Will you tell me a story,
please? Listening to
stories makes me feel
sleepy."

Mommy settled Ethan on her lap,
and he snuggled up close.

She told him stories
about all the funny things
she had done when she
was little—just like him.

"Sometimes I didn't feel
tired at bedtime either,"
Mommy said.

Mommy carried Ethan back inside. She smiled a secret smile as she remembered how her mommy used to put her to bed when she was little.

Mommy tucked Ethan into bed. She pulled the covers right up to his nose.

"My mommy used to tuck me into bed with the blankets pulled right up to my nose—like this!" she said.

"Then she'd stroke the top of my head—like this," Mommy said.

Very gently, she stroked the top of Ethan's head.
"And she'd give me a special kiss good night," said Mommy.

She gave Ethan a very special kiss good night.

"What next, Mommy?" said Ethan, with a big yawn.

"And then she'd say, 'Good night, sleep tight!'" said Mommy.

"Good night, Mommy," yawned Ethan . . . .

But before Mommy could say, "Sleep tight," Ethan was fast asleep!